Dust Devil

by

ANNE ISAACS

illustrated by

PAUL O. ZELINSKY

schwartz **&** wade books · new york

For Amy, with all my love—A.I.

For Anna in the Marshall Islands—*jen yokwe eo elap ilo n̄a*—P.O.Z.

The author wishes to thank Todd Harvey and the American Folklife Center at the Library of Congress for their help.

Text copyright © 2010 by The Anne Isaacs 2004 Trust • Illustrations copyright © 2010 by Paul O. Zelinsky • All rights reserved. • Published in the United States by Schwartz & Wade Books, an imprint of Random House Children's Books, a division of Random House, Inc., New York. • Schwartz & Wade Books and the colophon are trademarks of Random House, Inc. • Visit us on the Web! www.randomhouse.com/kids • Educators and librarians, for a variety of teaching tools, visit us at www.randomhouse.com/teachers • *Library of Congress Cataloging-in-Publication Data* • Isaacs, Anne. • Dust devil / by Anne Isaacs ; illustrated by Paul O. Zelinsky.—1st ed. • p. cm. • Summary: Having moved to Montana from Tennessee in the 1830s, fearless Angelica Longrider—also known as Swamp Angel—changes the state's landscape, tames a wild horse, and captures some desperadoes. • ISBN 978-0-375-86722-4—ISBN 978-0-375-96722-1 (glb) • [1. Frontier and pioneer life—Montana—Fiction. 2. Montana—History—19th century—Fiction. 3. Tall tales.] I. Zelinsky, Paul O, ill. II. Title. • PZ7.I762Dus 2010 • [Fic]—dc22 • 2009040877 • Random House Children's Books supports the First Amendment and celebrates the right to read.

The text of this book is set in CG Cloister. • The illustrations were painted in oils on cedar, aspen, and maple veneers.

MANUFACTURED IN CHINA
2 4 6 8 10 9 7 5 3 1
First Edition

★ NOTICE ★

WHAT YOU ARE ABOUT TO READ

IS A GENUINE

MONTANA STORY.

ON THIS EARTH, ONLY ONE
THING IS AS RELIABLE AS A
MONTANA STORY, AND THAT'S A

MONTANA FENCE POST:

EITHER OF THEM MAY

LEAN A LITTLE,
BUT THEY SELDOM

FLAT-OUT LIE.

Unless you've read a book
called *Swamp Angel*, you may not know about
Angelica Longrider, or how she got the nickname
Swamp Angel, and a reputation as the wildest wildcat
in Tennessee. The way that book ends up is this . . .

When Swamp Angel grew too big for Tennessee, she
moved west to Montana, a country so sizeable that
even Angel could fit in. And back in 1831,
Montana was nearly perfect.

Still, Angel had to make a few adjustments. To start with, the sun woke her three hours earlier than it had in Tennessee. Angel looked out her window, trying to figure it out.

To the east the land was flatter than a fry pan. To the north it was flatter than a flapjack in a fry pan. To the south it was flatter than butter melting on a flapjack in a fry pan. It didn't take long to see what was missing: shade!

She began to feel homesick for Tennessee, where trees grow so thick that deer have to take off their antlers to get through the forest. With all that shade, the sun couldn't wake a body until she was good and ready.

Then Angel looked west, where the Rocky Mountains stuck up halfway to the moon. "A ripe crop of shadows, if I ever seen one," says Angel.

She reached out, plucked the tallest mountain from the pack, and planted it east of her ranch, right where the sun was rising. Fast as a blink the sun disappeared, and didn't rise again for three hours.

Pretty soon all her neighbors wanted a mountain. So Angel grabbed an armful and planted mountains one by one on the prairie. "That's a beaut," she'd say proudly every time she set one down.

And to this day, every stand-alone peak in Montana is called a butte.

When Angel began to farm, she soon learned that Montana soil is rich enough to open its own bank. A seed planted at daybreak could be dangerous to bystanders before noon. One morning three cows wandered into Angel's cornfield at planting time. Some seedlings shot up and rocketed to the sky, taking the cows along for the ride. They weren't seen again until fall, when the stalks withered and lowered the cows back to earth.

The cows were none the worse for the trip, and the arrangement had its advantages, too: that whole summer it rained milk by the bucket.

But Angel's biggest problem was getting a horse. Oh, there were plenty of horses in Montana, but she could not find one powerful enough to carry her— until the summer of 1835, when the dust storm hit.

It was the worst storm
anyone had ever seen. Why, the
wind tore across Montana faster than a baby
ripping a newspaper. The sky got so full of dust
that it stayed dark day and night. Folks couldn't tell
whether to wake up or go to sleep, so they wore their
pajamas all the time.

Fields and orchards were
stripped bare. With winter coming on,
settlers were getting desperate. Aunt Essie Bell,
Angel's neighbor, baked endless platters of sourdough
biscuits for those in need. Unfortunately, so much dust got
into the batter that Essie's biscuits were hard as horseshoes,
and about as tasty.

When the dust storm
reached Angel's ranch, the wind
shrieked like a thousand trumpets
playing out of tune. The barn began
to shake, the ground to quake, the
windows to break, the animals to
wake, and everyone's ears to ache!
In the middle of the commotion,
Angel thought she heard a sound
like hooves pounding.

Then the gale blew
off the barn roof and
began to suck apples, oats,
and hay from their bins.
Angel got suspicious.

"Dust devil, it's time to
quit horsing around!" she
hollered, and without another
word she sprang right onto the back
of the whirlwind. The storm roared
and bellowed, tossing buckets, goats, and
pitchforks in every direction, and tried to throw
Angel off. Up into the sky she rode that bucking
blast, latching on for all she was worth.

"That the best you can do, blow-hard?" Angel
shouted into the gale. "Why, I've seen tumbleweed
bounce higher!"

Whenever they touched ground, Angel dug
her heels in, trying to slow the tempest down. Her
feet scraped out a long, winding ditch as they zigzagged
across the land. Nowadays, folks call it the Grand Canyon.
She rode the howling storm for two days and two nights.
On the third day it began to rain.

As the dust washed away, the black clouds faded to gray, then white, and finally cleared. And there, in the middle of the whirlwind, was a giant horse, bucking and wheeling and neighing like fury! Every time he struck his hooves together, bolts of lightning shot out.

Angel rode
the horse all the way
to the ground. By then he had
no more buck in him than a baby.
The minute he lay down, the wind dropped
and the sun shined for the first time in weeks.
"You'd make a fine sidekick," says Angel.
"I'll call you Dust Devil, and from now on we'll
ride together. I reckon I've finally found the
horse that can carry me."

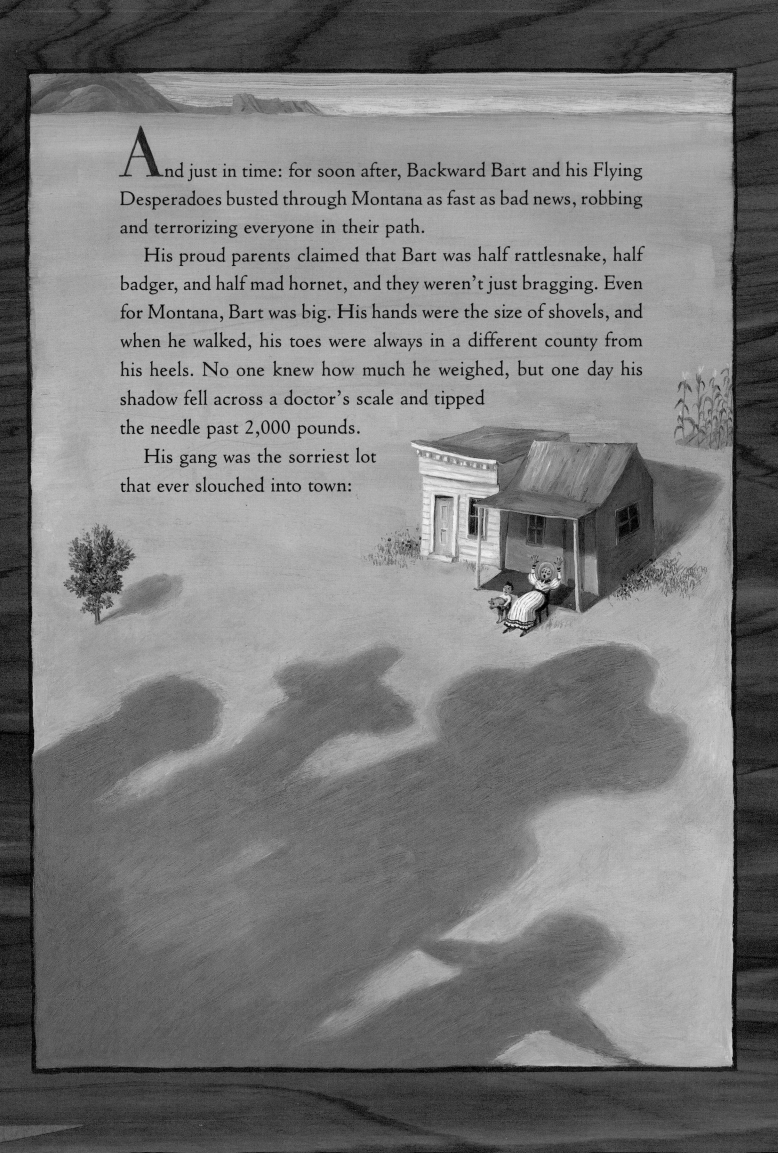

And just in time: for soon after, Backward Bart and his Flying Desperadoes busted through Montana as fast as bad news, robbing and terrorizing everyone in their path.

His proud parents claimed that Bart was half rattlesnake, half badger, and half mad hornet, and they weren't just bragging. Even for Montana, Bart was big. His hands were the size of shovels, and when he walked, his toes were always in a different county from his heels. No one knew how much he weighed, but one day his shadow fell across a doctor's scale and tipped the needle past 2,000 pounds.

His gang was the sorriest lot that ever slouched into town:

Bart and the Desperadoes were too ornery for any self-respecting horse to carry. So they rode mosquitoes.

Now, you may wonder at this, but it's a fact sworn to by everyone except newborns and Texans, that mosquitoes grow bigger in Montana than anywhere else. A Montana mosquito can carry a heavy suitcase and two watermelons on each wing without sweating. The Desperadoes' mosquitoes measured ten feet from mouth to tail, with stingers as long as swords. Bart's biting bandits could travel faster than a man on horseback, and a lot higher.

Bart's only problem was, he couldn't do anything forwards. You see, whenever his mother had wheeled baby Bart in his buggy, townsfolk fled at the sight. So the mayor issued a proclamation that Bart was never again to show his face in public.

From then on, his mother set Bart backwards in the buggy. He got so used to it that as he grew, he did everything—walking, talking, or flying—backwards.

Since he couldn't see where he was going, Bart sometimes landed in a manure heap or a pickle barrel. No one laughed at him. No one dared.

"Cash your gimme!" Backward Bart always shouted as he flew backwards into a farmer's yard, and no one waited for him to say "please." Bart's snarling sidekicks would hover around the farmer, aiming their swords at a tender spot on his backside.

"Up hurry!" Bart would shout, while the farmer emptied his piggy bank as fast as rain. Then the desperadoes would spur their mosquitoes and fly off calling, "Yap-giddy!"

When Swamp Angel heard about Bart, she mounted Dust Devil and paid a visit to Sheriff Napalot up in Billings. She found him snoring in the single-starred, double-barred, triple-guard jail.

"I'm here to help you catch the Flying Desperadoes," says Angel.

"I'm much obliged, Angel, but you can't do that," drawled the sheriff. "Only a member of my posse can hunt down outlaws. And the posse's already gone to get 'em."

"Then deputize me quick!"

"Well, dang it, Angel, to be deputized you have to be a man. It's the law."

"Tell me this, then: is there a law that says a woman can't catch a mosquito?"

"Well, I don't reckon—"

"Set the table, Sheriff; you'll have company for dinner!" Angel called as she rode off to find Backward Bart.

A few miles out of Billings, Angel discovered Sheriff Napalot's posse, unable to sit on their saddles. Seems they'd insulted the Desperadoes and got a stinging reply.

Angel chased Bart for a week; but everywhere she went, she arrived a day late.

So Angel stepped up on a mountaintop to get a better view. It wasn't hard to figure out where Bart had been, by the trail of broken piggy banks. "East to west, that's how he's doing it!" she declared. "Looks like Aunt Essie Bell's farm is next!"

"Won't you stay and have a biscuit?" Aunt Essie greeted Angel when she rode up.

"I'll save 'em for supper," says Angel; and she put the biscuits in her pocket. "Bart's coming, Essie. Grab your gold and hide!"

"Haven't got any gold except the fillings in my teeth," says Essie.

"Then grab your teeth and hide!" says Angel.

Essie didn't wait to hear it twice. She raced to her storm cellar
and locked the door just as Backward Bart sailed into her yard and
landed in the pigs' trough.

"Pee-yip!" he shouted, splashing happily in wormy oatmeal and
rotten eggs.

As the Desperadoes landed beside him, he prompted them, "Best the who's?"

"Best is Bart Backward!" they chanted, but they didn't look cheerful as they scraped moldy gravy from their beards.

"Varmints, give back the gold you've stolen, or prepare to fight!" says Angel.

"Huh?" says Bart.

"Fight to prepare or stolen, you've gold the back give, varmints!" Angel shouted. This time Bart understood.

Angel jumped on Dust Devil, who whirled up a storm and struck his hooves together, forging spears of lightning for Angel.

Faster than you can say "stinking stingers," the dripping Desperadoes mounted their mosquitoes. Angel hurled lightning, while they attacked from every direction.

Dust Devil blasted hot air from his nostrils with such force that he snorted the Desperadoes halfway to Kansas. But the gale nearly blew Angel off; and as she grabbed for the reins, she dropped her bolts of lightning. At once the Desperadoes moved in and aimed their mosquitoes. It didn't look good for Angel, up in that thicket of thorny thieves.

Then Swamp Angel remembered Aunt Essie's biscuits. She reached into her pocket and began to pelt the Desperadoes. To her surprise, the men dove for the rock-hard biscuits and gobbled them hungrily.

"More gimme!" they shouted. "Mee-*yum!*"

That gave Angel an idea. She headed east toward Billings, luring the Desperadoes with biscuits. Those greedy good-for-nothings followed her clear across Montana. But as they chomped on the biscuits, their teeth began to break off. The more they munched, the more teeth fell, heaping up in a jagged ridge on the ground below. Those hills are still called the Sawtooth Range.

Angel had just about
run out of biscuits, and the men
had run out of teeth, when they reached
Billings and the single-starred, double-
barred, triple-guard jail.
"Raise the roof, Dust Devil!" says Angel.
Then she set the last biscuit down on a table
and the Desperadoes sailed in after it.

"Wake up and lock the door,
Sheriff!" she shouted, while Dust
Devil clapped the roof back on.

When the Flying Desperadoes
realized they were in jail, they opened
their toothless mouths and bawled like babies.
Bart only laughed.
"Door the saw!" he ordered, and the Desperadoes
commenced to saw the door with their mosquitoes.

But quick as the stingers bored through, Dust
Devil hammered them down like bent nails.
Bart knew he was beat.

With Bart and his biting bandits behind bars, Angel returned to her ranch and tried to settle down. But every now and then Dust Devil got the wild jiggershanks and bolted from his corral. Sometimes he'd shave a cornfield balder than a parson before Angel could stop him. To this day in Montana, when a dust cloud whirls out of nowhere, with a wind that bellows like a horse, folks say that Dust Devil's broken loose again.

Since Montana law made no provision for sentencing insects, Bart's mosquitoes were allowed to go free; but they had been steered badly so long that they'd lost all sense of direction. As soon as those prodigious pests took to the air, they turned upside down and hit the ground drill end first—and got themselves into hot water. You can still see the geysers this gave rise to, any time you visit Montana.

Now, you may think
that Backward Bart and his
Flying Desperadoes never again set
folks on the run, but facts are otherwise.
It seems that when the Desperadoes dropped
their teeth, the gold fillings rolled out into mountain
springs and washed downstream, all the way to
California. Eventually settlers discovered
those nuggets and started a stampede.
But that's another story.